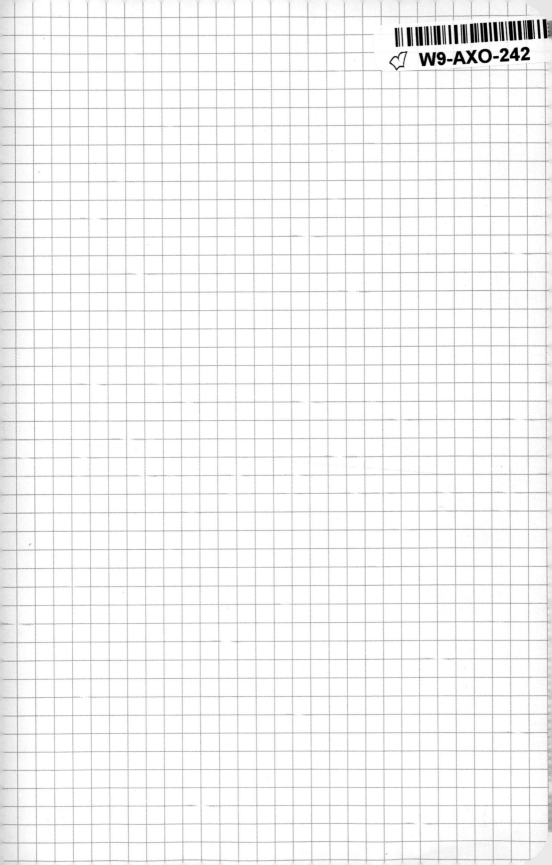

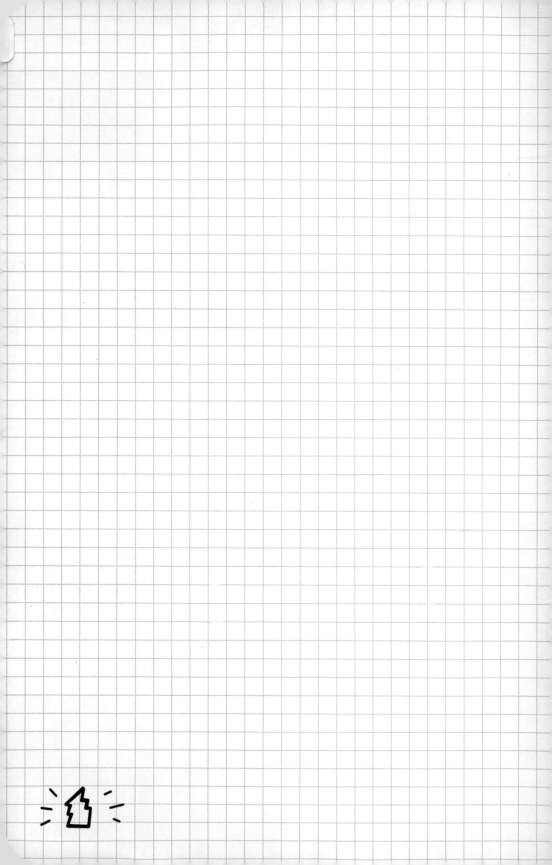

SHAZAM!

FREDDY'S GUIDE TO SUPER HERO-ING

ALL WORDS AND ART BY FREDDY FREEMAN

(WITH SOME HELP FROM STEVE BEHLING)

HARPER
An Imprint of HarperCollinsPublishers

Shazam! created by C.C. Beck and Bill Parker

Freddy's Guide to Super Hero-ing

Copyright © 2019 DC Comics

SHAZAM! and all related characters and elements © & ™ DC Comics and Warner Bros. Entertainment Inc.

(s19)

HARP41770

www.harpercollinschildrens.com

Library of Congress Control Number: 2018961963

ISBN 978-0-06-288418-3

Art by Leslie Design

Typography by Erica DeChavez

Editorial by Alexandra West

19 20 21 22 23   PC/LSCC   10 9 8 7 6 5 4 3 2 1

First Edition

CONTENTS

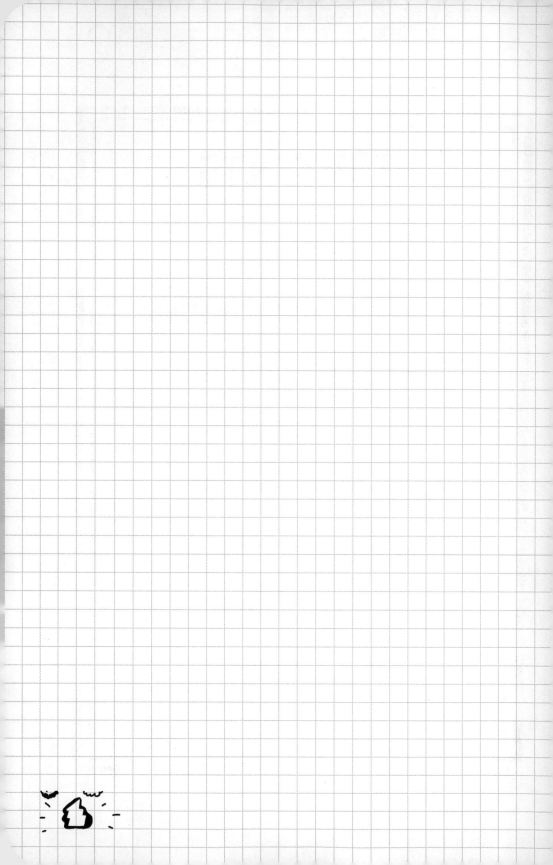

FREDDY'S GUIDE TO SUPER HERO-ING

DID YOU ANSWER YES? IF YOU DID, GOOD. THAT LETS ME KNOW HOW SMART YOU ARE, AND THAT YOU'RE REALLY GOING TO APPRECIATE WHAT YOU'RE ABOUT TO READ.

IF YOU DIDN'T ANSWER YES, THEN YOU SHOULD STOP READING THIS AND GO DO LITERALLY ANYTHING ELSE. BECAUSE WHAT YOU ARE ABOUT TO READ IS THE MOST EXCELLENT, MOST EXTRAORDINARY, MOST COMPREHENSIVE, BE-ALL, END-ALL JOURNAL EVER WRITTEN BY ME ABOUT SUPER HEROES.

OKAY, SO I HAVEN'T WRITTEN ANYTHING ELSE. AND IT'S NOT LIKE THIS IS A REAL, PUBLISHED BOOK OR ANYTHING. (YET! I HAD THIS THOUGHT THAT IF I WAS TO MAKE MY JOURNAL INTO A REAL BOOK, I WOULD HAVE TO WRITE IT LIKE IT WAS A BOOK, SO THAT'S WHAT I DID! I STARTED WRITING TO A READER! AND NOT JUST TO MYSELF. CAUSE THAT'S JUST WEIRD. "DEAR, ME ..." AWKWARD!) IT'S JUST MY JOURNAL. BUT SINCE IT IS MY JOURNAL, I CAN DO ANYTHING I WANT WITH IT. AND IF I SAY IT'S THE BEST JOURNAL EVER WRITTEN ABOUT SUPER HEROES, WELL, THEN THAT'S EXACTLY WHAT IT IS.

OH, ONE MORE THING. I ALSO MADE SOME QUIZZES THAT I PUT AT THE END OF EACH SECTION OF MY JOURNAL. I USE THESE TO TEST THE SUPER HERO KNOWLEDGE OF MY FRIENDS, SO I THOUGHT I'D PUT THEM IN HERE, TOO. IF YOU GET THEM ALL RIGHT, THEN MAYBE YOU NEED TO START A SUPER HERO JOURNAL OF YOUR OWN!

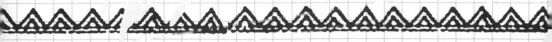

WHAT DOES IT TAKE TO BE A SUPER HERO?

THAT'S AN AWESOME QUESTION. AND IT'S REALLY HARD TO ANSWER. LIKE, YOU COULD JUST SAY THAT A SUPER HERO IS A SUPER HERO BECAUSE THEY HAVE INCREDIBLE POWERS AND ABILITIES.
BUT WHAT IF THEY USE THEM FOR EVIL, INSTEAD OF GOOD? OR WHAT IF THEY DECIDE TO DO NOTHING WITH THEIR POWERS, OR THEY JUST USE THEM TO MAKE THEIR DAILY LIVES A LITTLE EASIER, OR DO THEIR JOBS BETTER?

SEE? IT'S REALLY EASY TO GET AHEAD OF YOURSELF.
A SUPER HERO IS A SUPER HERO NOT BECAUSE OF THEIR POWERS, BUT BECAUSE OF WHO THEY ARE. THEY HAVE SOMETHING INSIDE THEM THAT MAKES THEM WANT TO HELP PEOPLE, TO USE THEIR ABILITIES TO DO SOME GOOD IN THE WORLD. IT SOUNDS CORNY, I KNOW. BUT IT'S THE TRUTH.

TAKE A LOOK AT **SUPERMAN**. NO, REALLY, LOOK. I PUT HIS PICTURE HERE AND EVERYTHING.

ZOOM!!!

WHAT MAKES SUPERMAN TICK?

THAT'S **ANOTHER** REALLY GOOD QUESTION. MAN, I'M REALLY GOOD AT WRITING. ANYWAY. WHAT MAKES SUPERMAN, UH, SUPERMAN? LIKE, WHY DOES HE DO THE THINGS HE DOES? I THINK UNDERSTANDING THAT IS A BIG STEP TOWARD FIGURING OUT WHAT MAKES A SUPER HERO.

CHECKLIST

- ✓ FIGHTS FOR TRUTH AND JUSTICE
- ✓ INSPIRES OTHERS
- ✓ STANDS UP AGAINST THE BULLIES OF THE WORLD
- ✓ WON'T EVER GIVE UP
- ✓ CARES ABOUT EVERYONE

WHAT MAKES SUPERMAN SO SUPER???

THAT'S A SILLY QUESTION. I KNOW I ASKED IT BUT IT IS STILL A VERY SILLY QUESTION.

EVERYTHING ABOUT SUPERMAN MAKES HIM SUPER, FROM HIS POWERS TO HIS MORALITY TO EVEN HIS COOL SUIT.

HOW DO YOU KNOW ALL THIS STUFF?

BECAUSE THEY WRITE A TON OF GREAT ARTICLES ABOUT HIM IN THE *DAILY PLANET*. AND BY "THEY," I MEAN LOIS LANE. I'M A BIG FAN. I'D DO ANYTHING TO PICK HER BRAIN.

I WRITE LETTERS TO THE *DAILY PLANET* PRETTY REGULARLY, AND I ASK ALL SORTS OF QUESTIONS ABOUT SUPERMAN, AND SUPER HEROES IN GENERAL. AND WHILE I DON'T ALWAYS GET A RESPONSE (AND WHEN I DO, IT'S NOT USUALLY FROM LOIS LANE), SOMEBODY THERE DOES TAKE THE TIME TO WRITE BACK AND ANSWER ALL MY QUESTIONS. WHICH IS AWESOME.

I WROTE TO THE *DAILY PLANET* PRETTY RECENTLY TO ASK IF I COULD MAYBE WRITE AN ARTICLE MYSELF SINCE (AS YOU'LL SOON FIND OUT) I'M PRETTY MUCH A SHAZAM EXPERT. FINGERS CROSSED THEY WRITE BACK!!!

Planet

SPECIAL EDITION

JUSTICE LEAG
HEROES AMONG

By Lois Lane

This is what we know. The world has grown darker and while we have reason to fear, we have the strength not to. There are heroes among us to remind us that only from fear comes courage, that only from the darkness can we truly feel the light. Darkness, the truest darkness, is not the absence of light. It is the conviction that the light will never return. But the light always returns to show us things familiar—home, family—and things entire[ly] new, or long overlooked. [It] shows us new possibilities a[nd] challenges us to pursue the[m]. This time, the light shone [on] the heroes coming out of t[he] shadows to tell us we won't [be] alone again. Our darkness w[as] deep and soon to swallow a[ll] hope. But these heroes we[re] here the whole time to remi[nd] us that hope is real. That yo[u] can see it. All you have to d[o] is look, up in the sky.

SUPER HERO PERKS

BEING A SUPER HERO APPARENTLY GETS YOU A TOY DEAL. CHECK IT OUT! I FOUND THESE AWESOME (TOTALLY NOT GEEKY) BATMAN TOYS AT THE MALL. BATMAN HAS TOYS. AND SLIPPERS! SLIPPERS. REALLY,

DARK KNIGHT?

I DON'T WANT TO BRAG (BUT I WILL) I DO HAVE THE SUPERMAN LIMITED-EDITION 100% OFFICIAL SNAPBACK. ONE SIZE FITS MOST. AND I AM MOST.

SUPER HERO SYMBOLS

SUPERMAN

STRANGE VISITOR FROM ANOTHER PLANET. FASTER THAN
A SPEEDING BULLET, MORE POWERFUL THAN A LOCOMOTIVE,
AND ABLE TO LEAP TALL BUILDINGS IN A SINGLE BOUND.

BATMAN

THE DARK KNIGHT.
THE CAPED CRUSADER.
A CRIMINAL'S WORST
NIGHTMARE. BUT
BENEATH THAT
BROODING BAT SYMBOL
IS A BIG HEART, TOO.
AT LEAST I HOPE SO.

WONDER WOMAN

WARRIOR. PRINCESS.
AMBASSADOR.
WONDER WOMAN
IS LIKE A BRIGHT,
SHINING BEACON
OF HOPE. SHE HAS
SUCH COMPASSION
AND EMPATHY FOR
EVERYONE.

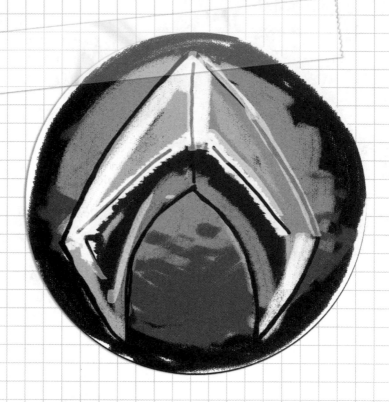

AQUAMAN

PART HUMAN. PART ATLANTEAN. ALL HERO. THIS IS ONE WARRIOR WHO GOES BY HIS REAL NAME, ARTHUR CURRY. LIKE, EVERYONE KNOWS WHO HE IS. UNLIKE, SAY, BATMAN OR SUPERMAN, WHO HAVE SECRET IDENTITIES. ASK ANY PERSON ON THE STREET, "HEY, WHO IS THE AQUAMAN?" AND THEY'LL SAY, "ARTHUR CURRY!"

CYBORG

Is he man? Is he machine? Or is he both? If you said "both," then you're exactly right. Cyborg (not sure of his real name) seems to be a combination of the mechanical and the human.

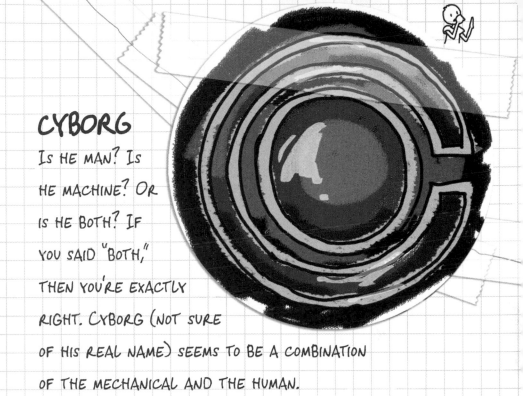

THE FLASH

Some call him "The Fastest Man Alive." Some call him "The Scarlet Speedster." Either way, he's fast. How fast? He can run on top of water! ON. TOP. OF. WATER. You know what happens if YOU or ME try running on the top of water? We sink.

SUPER-VILLAINS!

A SUPER HERO'S KEY JOB RESPONSIBILITY IS PROBABLY CATCHING BAD GUYS, AKA VILLAINS, AND THAT INCLUDES SUPER-VILLAINS. BUT WHAT MAKES A SUPER-VILLAIN? WELL, BAD EXPERIENCES, TROUBLED UPBRINGINGS, MYSTICAL SUPERPOWERS THAT BASICALLY DRIVE YOU INSANE. THE USUAL. BUT IT'S A SUPER HERO'S JOB TO CATCH AND BRING TO JUSTICE ANYONE WHO BREAKS THE LAW.

I'M LOOKING AT YOU, LEX LUTHOR.

THE JOKER

HA HA HA HA

HERE ARE SOME OF THE BADDEST OF THE BAD:

LEX LUTHOR (OBVIOUSLY)
GENERAL ZOD
THE JOKER
HARLEY QUINN
DOOMSDAY

SUPER-QUIZ #1

My friend Billy had a great idea. He said I could include quizzes at the end of each section of my super hero book so anyone who reads it can test themselves to see how much they've learned. At first that sounded a lot like school to me, but then I thought that it could be cool. See, Billy and I don't really like school. When Billy came to live at the foster home with us, he became one of the family. He's a bit of a "troubled" kid with a "dark" past but it doesn't "bother" me. We get along "great." Am I using these quotes right? Anyway, he's one of my best buds now, so I trust him when it comes to this sort of stuff. So here's the first quiz. See how you do!

1. WHO IS FASTER, SUPERMAN OR THE FLASH? (IN MY OPINION)
   A. SUPERMAN
   B. THE FLASH
   C. EVEN SUPERMAN DOESN'T KNOW

2. WHAT DOESN'T IT TAKE TO BE A SUPER HERO?

   A. WON'T EVER GIVE UP
   B. INSPIRES OTHERS
   C. ABILITY TO SHOOT MILK OUT OF YOUR NOSE.

ANSWERS: 1. b, 2. c

SCORING:

0 CORRECT: YOU'D BETTER REREAD SECTION 1.

1 CORRECT: PRETTY GOOD. MOVE ON TO SECTION 2, FELLOW HERO!

2 CORRECT: HOW IS THAT EVEN POSSIBLE?

SECTION 2

THE FREDDY FREEMAN COLLECTION

You already know that I read everything about super heroes that I can get my hands on. Even stuff I can't get my hands on. Wait, that makes no sense. But it kinda does. Anyway. And I think you already have an idea that I collect super hero memorabilia, too. I have some pretty special stuff in my collection. And for the first time, I want to share it with everyone.

THE DAILY PLANET ARCHIVE

Gotham

Daily

★★★ EXTRA ★★★

Man of Steel Strik
HUNDREDS S

Plan

SPECIAL EDITION

WONDER WO
BULLETS AND GAU

Daily Planet

SPECIAL EDITION

BATMAN
Guardian in Metropolis?

Aga... ...ETS ...

AVED

MAN
LETS

WHEN I FIRST STARTED GETTING
INTO SUPER HEROES, MY GO-TO
SOURCE WAS THE DAILY PLANET.
AT FIRST, I USED TO GO TO THE
WEBSITE. I STILL DO, EVERY DAY.
BUT WHEN I BEGAN COLLECTING,
I WANTED HARD COPIES. SO I WOULD
GET THE ACTUAL NEWSPAPER, AND
CUT OUT THE HEADLINES
AND ARTICLES.

MY COLLECTION IS PRETTY
IMPRESSIVE, IF I DO SAY SO MYSELF!

THE REFERENCE LIBRARY

After I got into the *Daily Planet*, I really wanted to know everything there was to know about super heroes. So I put together my own super hero library. I got these books from thrift stores, garage sales, auctions, wherever I could find them. Some of them are pretty rare!

The Hero Inside

An Exmaination into the Self and Identity

The Twenty-First-Century Superhuman: *Essays on Gender Identity in a New Era*

Biopolitics
in the Age of
Meta-Humans

★ ★ ★

JUSTICE
LEAGUE:
GODS
AMONG
MEN

THE
MYSTERY
OF
ATLANTIS

SHAZAM!

FREDDY'S
GUIDE TO
SUPER HERO-ING

OKAY, SO THIS ONE
ISN'T REAL. BUT MAYBE
ONE DAY IT WILL BE!

ART GALLERY

CLASSIC!

SPEEDY!

POWERFUL!

CYBORG-Y!

I DON'T CLAIM TO BE AN AMAZING ARTIST OR ANYTHING, BUT I'M NOT HALF BAD, EITHER. SOMETIMES I LIKE TO SIT AND DRAW SUPER HEROES. I THINK IT HELPS ME TO UNDERSTAND THEM A LITTLE BETTER.

FISHY!

SPOOKY!

SHAZAMAZING!

"THE SECRET
SHELVES"

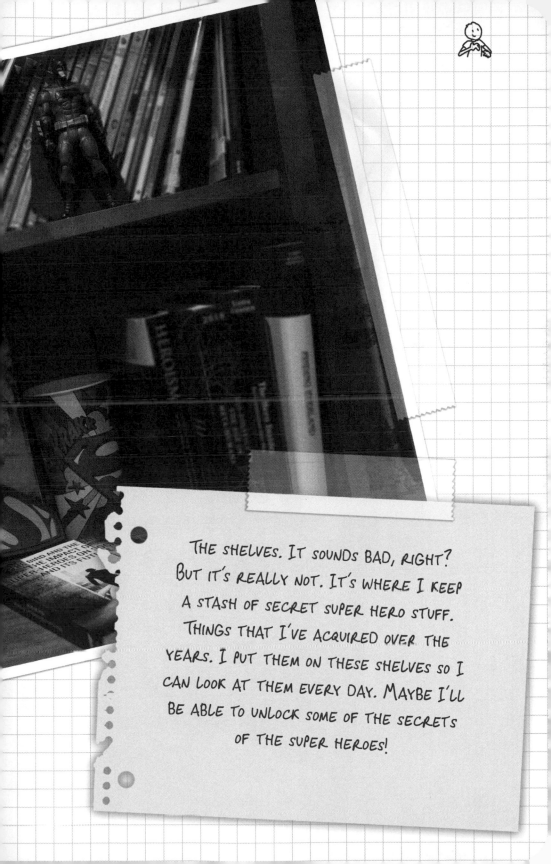

THE SHELVES. IT SOUNDS BAD, RIGHT?
BUT IT'S REALLY NOT. IT'S WHERE I KEEP
A STASH OF SECRET SUPER HERO STUFF.
THINGS THAT I'VE ACQUIRED OVER THE
YEARS. I PUT THEM ON THESE SHELVES SO I
CAN LOOK AT THEM EVERY DAY. MAYBE I'LL
BE ABLE TO UNLOCK SOME OF THE SECRETS
OF THE SUPER HEROES!

COLLECTIBLE CUPS

Okay, these are just straight-up cool. So a few years back, when Superman was fighting Zod's evil Kryptonian forces, the battle raged throughout a small town called, uh, Smallville. There was terrible destruction as a result of the fight, and one of the town's convenience stores was almost wiped off the map. Except it wasn't, because Superman saved it. They commemorated the event with these cool cups!

"ZODS" AND ENDS

I'M SORRY, I COULDN'T RESIST THAT ONE. I'VE FOUND A LOT OF INTERESTING ITEMS IN MY TIME AS A SUPER HERO EXPERT. THESE ARE JUST A FEW OF THE MORE INTERESTING, RARE, AND ONE-OF-A-KIND THINGS IN MY COLLECTION.

MIRROR

THIS USED TO BE PART OF A CAR, BEFORE IT WAS FLATTENED WHEN ZOD ATTACKED METROPOLIS.

RUSTY JAIL BAR

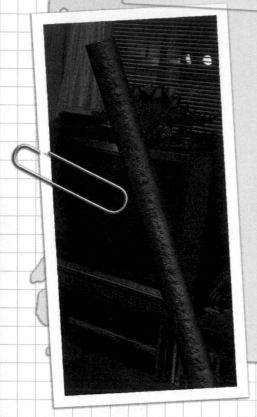

SURE, IT MAY LOOK LIKE JUST A RUSTY OLD BAR THAT WAS IN A JAIL CELL. AND IT IS. I MEAN, IT WAS. WELL, YOU GET THE POINT. BUT IT'S ALSO SPECIAL BECAUSE IT COMES FROM STRYKER'S ISLAND, THE PRISON WHERE BATMAN, SUPERMAN, AND WONDER WOMAN FOUGHT A BATTLE AGAINST SOME BIZARRE CREATURE.

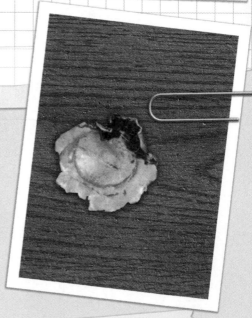

BULLET

THIS BABY BOUNCED RIGHT OFF SUPERMAN'S CHEST (THAT'S WHY IT'S FLAT AS A PANCAKE NOW). IT'S A KEEPER.

SUPERMAN'S CORN CHIPS

THIS ONE IS EXACTLY WHAT YOU THINK IT IS. IT'S A BAG OF CORN CHIPS THAT COMES DIRECTLY FROM THE SMALLVILLE CONVENIENCE STORE THAT SUPERMAN SAVED IN THAT BIG BATTLE WITH ZOD'S EVIL KRYPTONIAN FORCES I WAS TELLING YOU ABOUT. NOW, I DON'T KNOW FOR SURE IF IT'S REALLY FROM THAT STORE. I GOT IT FROM AN ONLINE AUCTION SITE. THE SELLER HAS A 99% RATING, SO I'M BETTING IT'S LEGIT.

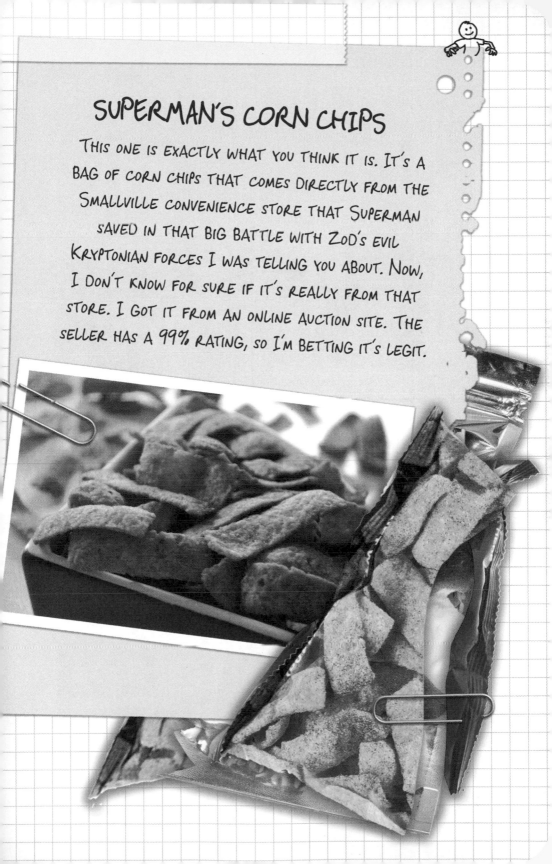

THE FAM

THIS WOULD USUALLY GO IN MY AUTHOR BIO AT THE END OF THE BOOK, BUT I MIGHT AS WELL PUT IT HERE. IT IS MY BOOK AFTER ALL. THIS IS MY FOSTER FAMILY. LOVE 'EM. HATE 'EM. PRANK 'EM. THEY ARE HERE TO STAY AND THAT'S PRETTY SUPER.

(CHEESY I KNOW.)

EXCUSE THE MESS. DARLA GOT AHOLD OF MY NOTEBOOK AGAIN!

DARLA IS MY LITTLE FOSTER SISTER. SHE'S COOL I GUESS—SHE ALWAYS SAYS I'M HER REAL BROTHER AND HUGS ME A LOT. SO I LET THE GLITTER SLIDE.

DARLA

SUPER-QUIZ #2

How well do you know my museum of awesome super hero stuff?

1. Which of the following items is NOT a part of Freddy's collection?
   A. A car mirror
   B. A floor tile crushed by Zod
   C. A flattened bullet

2. WHAT'S THE STORY BEHIND THE COLLECTIBLE SUPERMAN CUPS?

> A. THEY WERE MADE TO CELEBRATE SUPERMAN'S BIRTHDAY.
>
> B. THEY WERE MADE TO CELEBRATE SUPERMAN'S NEW HAIRCUT.
>
> C. THEY WERE MADE TO CELEBRATE A CONVENIENCE STORE THAT SUPERMAN SAVED.

3. WHAT'S BETTER, POTATO CHIPS OR CORN CHIPS?

> A. POTATO CHIPS
>
> B. CORN CHIPS
>
> C. THEY'RE BOTH PRETTY GOOD.

ANSWERS: 1. B, 2. C, 3. A, B, OR C—IT DEPENDS ON YOUR TASTE, REALLY.

0–1 CORRECT: TAKE ANOTHER TOUR OF THE MUSEUM!

2 CORRECT: YOU MIGHT MAKE A FINE TOUR GUIDE!

3 CORRECT: YOU'RE READY TO START YOUR OWN SUPER HERO ARCHIVE!

SHAZAM!

OHMYGOSHOHMY GOSHOHMYGOSH OHMYGOSH

I JUST MET A REAL LIVE

SUPER HERO!!!!!

A NEW SUPER HERO. LIKE BRAND-NEW. HE HAS NO TOYS OR SOCIAL MEDIA. NOTHING! BRAND-NEW. AND HIS NAME IS SHAZAM AND HE IS MY BEST FRIEND!!

OKAY, OKAY, OKAY, I KNOW. YOU'VE GOT A LOT OF QUESTIONS. WELL, DON'T YOU WORRY, I'M GONNA ANSWER THEM.

WHAT DOES "SHAZAM" MEAN, ANYWAY?

THAT'S A GREAT QUESTION. IT'S NOT LIKE YOU HEAR THE NAME SHAZAM EVERY DAY. IT DOES SOUND COOL, THOUGH. BUT WHAT DOES IT MEAN? Y'KNOW, LIKE THE NAME FREDDY. IT COMES FROM FREDERICK. IT MEANS "PEACEFUL RULER." WHICH I'M NOT. I MEAN, I'M PEACEFUL, BUT I'M NOT A RULER. BUT I DO KINDA RULE. ANYWAY.

HERE'S WHAT SHAZAM ACTUALLY STANDS FOR:

S — THE WISDOM OF SOLOMON

H — THE STRENGTH OF HERCULES

A — THE STAMINA OF ATLAS

Z — THE POWER OF ZEUS

A — THE COURAGE OF ACHILLES

M — THE FLIGHT (AND SPEED) OF MERCURY

HOW DID SHAZAM BECOME SHAZAM?

IT'S KIND OF A LONG, WEIRD STORY, AND I'M NOT EVEN SURE IF I BELIEVE IT. BUT THERE WAS THIS PERSON, A REGULAR PERSON, LIKE YOU OR ME. AND HE STUMBLED UPON AN ANCIENT WIZARD, WHOSE NAME WAS ALSO SHAZAM. THIS WIZARD SUPPOSEDLY LIVED AT A PLACE THAT'S FAR AWAY FROM EARTH, CALLED THE ROCK OF ETERNITY. IT'S IN SPACE, OR ANOTHER DIMENSION, OR SOMETHING LIKE THAT. PUT IT THIS WAY—IT'S NOT LIKE YOU CAN JUST HOP ON THE BUS OR SUBWAY AND GET THERE. OR MAYBE YOU CAN . . . ? IT'S A LITTLE CONFUSING.

SO THIS WIZARD WHO I MENTIONED BEFORE? HE WAS LOOKING FOR A CHAMPION, SOMEONE WHO HE COULD GIVE HIS POWER TO. AND THIS PERSON WAS WORTHY. SHAZAM KNEW THAT THEY WOULD USE ALL THOSE ABILITIES FOR GOOD, NOT FOR THEIR OWN SELFISH ENDS. SO SHAZAM BESTOWED THAT POWER TO THIS PERSON, AND THEY BECAME SHAZAM. A CHAMPION.

WAIT, SO THE **WIZARD** WAS NAMED SHAZAM, TOO?

BOY, YOU SURE ASK A LOT OF QUESTIONS! YES, THE WIZARD WAS NAMED SHAZAM. AND THE SUPER HERO, MY FRIEND, THE ONE WHO MAYBE CAN FLY FASTER THAN SUPERMAN? HE'S ALSO SHAZAM. SO, YES, THERE ARE—WERE—TWO SHAZAMS. THAT'S BECAUSE, ACCORDING TO THE SUPER HERO, THE WIZARD SHAZAM IS NO MORE. HE DIDN'T SAY MUCH BEYOND THAT, BUT I THINK IT'S A PRETTY BIG LOSS NOT JUST FOR HIM, BUT FOR THE WORLD.

SAME NAME, DIFFERENT GUY

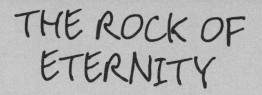

THE ROCK OF ETERNITY

No, NOT THE BAND FROM THE '80s.
THE MAGICAL REALM WHERE SHAZAM RECEIVED HIS
MAGICAL POWERS FROM THE WIZARD. WHAT IS IT
EXACTLY? WELL, I'VE NEVER BEEN THERE. I ASKED
SHAZAM TO TAKE ME AND HE WAS LIKE
NO! NO! NO! IMPOSSIBLE.
I'D BASICALLY DISINTEGRATE,
BUT . . . SHAZAM DID SNAP A QUICK PICTURE
BEFORE HE ZAPPED OUT OF THERE!

THE WISDOM OF SOLOMON

So, who is Solomon? Well, according to the ever-knowing and all-true internet, Solomon was the biblical king most famous for his wisdom. Just HOW did he get this wisdom you ask (or didn't ask, but I'm going to tell you anyway)? Well, he ASKED for it. You see, God (THE God, not like a super god or a demigod) appeared in a dream Solomon was having. God asked Solomon if he could have AAAAAAAAnything in the world, what would it be? And Solomon said "wisdom." Which is much better than let's say, minutes for your phone. Or likes on your social media page. WISDOM. Which is not something physical, and unlike something physical, wisdom is forever. Because it is knowledge, tied to experience, the spirit, and universe stuff. Again, internet said this. I have to believe it. Which makes sense. If I could have anything, I get why wisdom would be a good ask. Unless it's the Batmobile. Batmobile first. THEN wisdom.

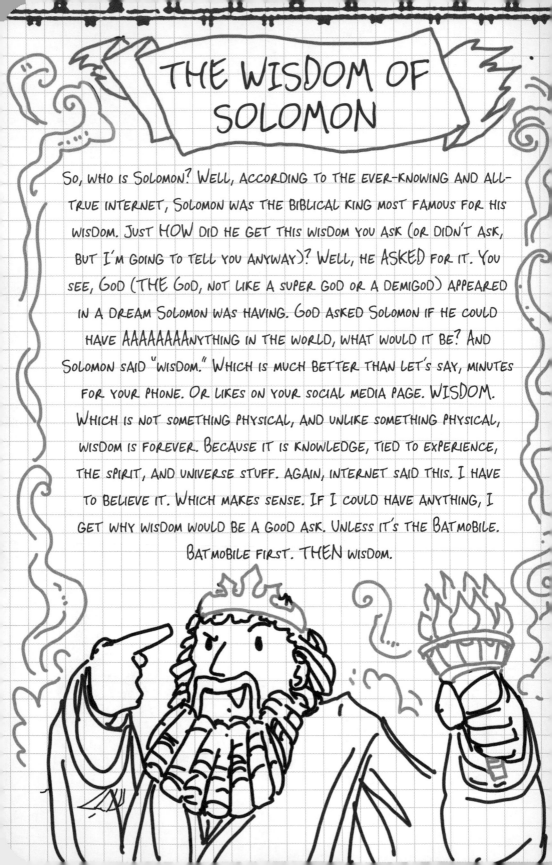

THE STRENGTH OF HERCULES

He was famous for his strength, his many adventures to faraway lands and worlds, and apparently suffering. Some crazy lady god cast a spell on Herc. Herc went crazy. Did bad things. Spell broke. Herc felt guilty for the bad things he did. Ran to the God of Truth and Healing, Apollo. Asked for help. Apollo promised Herc that if he endured a lot of pain and suffering in his lifetime (google "Hercules 12 heroic labors" for more info), he'd let Herc live forever amongst the gods on Mount Olympus.

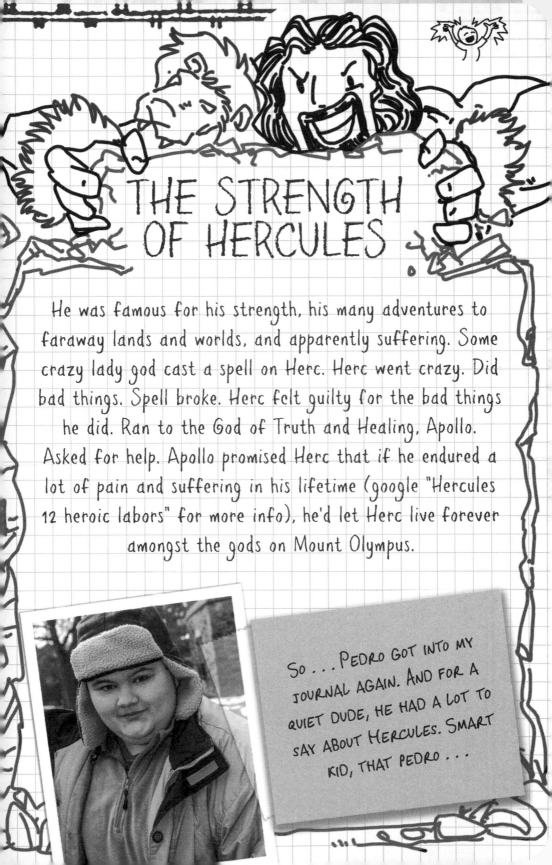

So... Pedro got into my journal again. And for a quiet dude, he had a lot to say about Hercules. Smart kid, that Pedro...

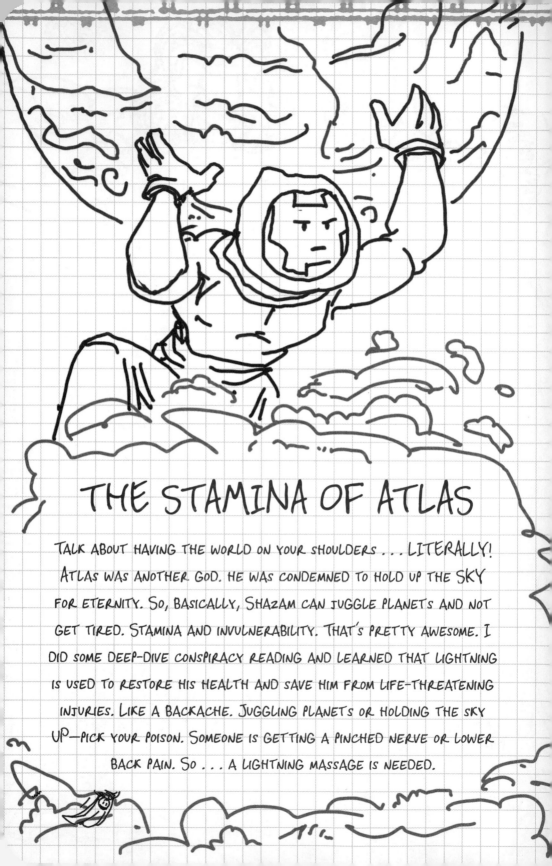

THE STAMINA OF ATLAS

TALK ABOUT HAVING THE WORLD ON YOUR SHOULDERS . . . LITERALLY!
ATLAS WAS ANOTHER GOD. HE WAS CONDEMNED TO HOLD UP THE SKY
FOR ETERNITY. SO, BASICALLY, SHAZAM CAN JUGGLE PLANETS AND NOT
GET TIRED. STAMINA AND INVULNERABILITY. THAT'S PRETTY AWESOME. I
DID SOME DEEP-DIVE CONSPIRACY READING AND LEARNED THAT LIGHTNING
IS USED TO RESTORE HIS HEALTH AND SAVE HIM FROM LIFE-THREATENING
INJURIES. LIKE A BACKACHE. JUGGLING PLANETS OR HOLDING THE SKY
UP—PICK YOUR POISON. SOMEONE IS GETTING A PINCHED NERVE OR LOWER
BACK PAIN. SO . . . A LIGHTNING MASSAGE IS NEEDED.

THE POWER OF ZEUS

OK. So I think SHAZAM MIGHT really be Zeus.
See below. JUST SAYIN'!

Zeus is known for the following symbols: thunderbolt, eagle, bull, and the oak tree. (What would his Super Hero name be if it was a combo of eagle, bull, and oak tree? Captain EagleBullTree.) Zeus was the king of the Greek gods, who lived on Mount Olympus. He was the god of the sky and thunder. Zeus was the mightiest of the Greek gods and had a number of powers. His most famous power is the ability to throw lightning bolts. (SEE! There it is again! The lightning bolt!) His winged horse Pegasus carried his lightning bolts and he trained an eagle to retrieve them. (Ignore this flying horse/eagle talk.) He could also control the weather, causing rain and huge storms.
(Dude, instant snow day!)
Oh, apparently Zeus could talk to animals and turn people into animals if he wanted to, which just sounds so NOT like a cool superpower. But if ya think about it, if you went to the zoo, and you didn't like someone that was also at the zoo? Instant flying poop show.

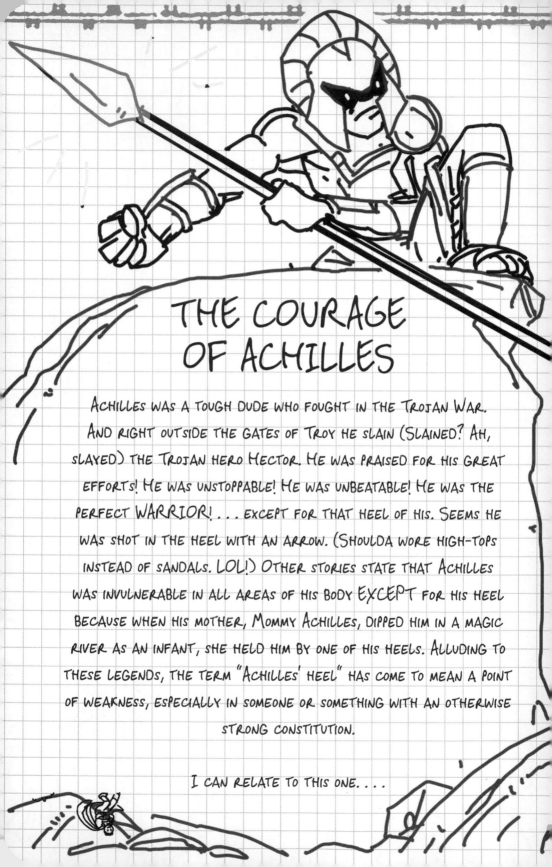

THE COURAGE OF ACHILLES

ACHILLES WAS A TOUGH DUDE WHO FOUGHT IN THE TROJAN WAR. AND RIGHT OUTSIDE THE GATES OF TROY HE SLAIN (SLAINED? AH, SLAYED) THE TROJAN HERO HECTOR. HE WAS PRAISED FOR HIS GREAT EFFORTS! HE WAS UNSTOPPABLE! HE WAS UNBEATABLE! HE WAS THE PERFECT WARRIOR! . . . EXCEPT FOR THAT HEEL OF HIS. SEEMS HE WAS SHOT IN THE HEEL WITH AN ARROW. (SHOULDA WORE HIGH-TOPS INSTEAD OF SANDALS. LOL!) OTHER STORIES STATE THAT ACHILLES WAS INVULNERABLE IN ALL AREAS OF HIS BODY EXCEPT FOR HIS HEEL BECAUSE WHEN HIS MOTHER, MOMMY ACHILLES, DIPPED HIM IN A MAGIC RIVER AS AN INFANT, SHE HELD HIM BY ONE OF HIS HEELS. ALLUDING TO THESE LEGENDS, THE TERM "ACHILLES' HEEL" HAS COME TO MEAN A POINT OF WEAKNESS, ESPECIALLY IN SOMEONE OR SOMETHING WITH AN OTHERWISE STRONG CONSTITUTION.

I CAN RELATE TO THIS ONE. . . .

THE SPEED OF MERCURY

WOW. SO MERCURY IS APPARENTLY FAST.
LIKE, REALLY FAST.

MERCURY SPEEDS AROUND THE SUN EVERY
LIKE 88 DAYS, TRAVELING THROUGH SPACE
AT NEARLY

112,000 MPH.

(BET THE BATMOBILE CAN'T DO THAT!)

WHAT CAN HE DO WITH THE POWERS OF ALL THOSE GUYS?

ANOTHER EXCELLENT QUESTION. I'VE BEEN WORKING WITH MY GOOD FRIEND SHAZAM (I DID MENTION WE'RE FRIENDS, RIGHT?) TO FIGURE OUT THAT EXACT THING. SO FAR, WE'VE DISCOVERED A FEW OF HIS POWERS. THERE MIGHT EVEN BE MORE, WHICH IS PRETTY EXCITING!

STRENGTH

OBVS, WE KNOW WHAT "STRENGTH OF HERCULES" MEANS. IT MEANS HE'S STRONG LIKE HERCULES! NOT THE HERCULES FROM SOME MOVIE OR BOOK OR LEGEND, EITHER. LIKE, THE REAL HERCULES. SO HOW STRONG IS THAT? TRY LIFTING-CARS STRONG. CATCHING-PARTS-OF-A-BUILDING-IN-HIS-BARE-HANDS STRONG.

SPEED

SHAZAM CAN MOVE. FAST. I'M NOT SURE IF HE CAN MOVE FLASH FAST. BUT HE'S DEFINITELY FASTER THAN BATMAN'S BATMOBILE—IN HER ARTICLE "BAT-TECH: AN OUTSIDE LOOK AT THE GADGETS AND GEAR OF THE DARK KNIGHT," LOIS LANE ESTIMATED THE BATMOBILE'S TOP SPEED AT TWO HUNDRED MILES PER HOUR.

FLIGHT

JUST LIKE SUPERMAN (OR MERCURY), SHAZAM CAN CRUISE THROUGH THE SKY. FASTER THAN A SPEEDING BULLET, YOU KNOW THE DRILL. I WOULD LOVE TO KNOW WHO COULD FLY FASTER OR HIGHER, THOUGH. MAYBE SOMETHING TO LOOK INTO.

SUPERPOWER TEST IDEAS

List what powers you think I should test. I need some help brainstorming!

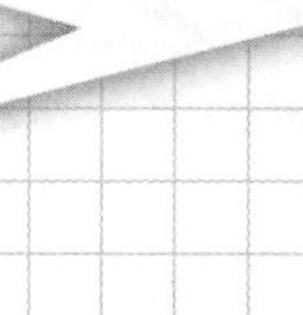

_____

_____

_____

_____

_____

_____

_____

_____

_____

WHY DOES SHAZAM WEAR A CAPE?

IF YOU ASKED SHAZAM (THE WIZARD, NOT THE HERO), I BET HE WOULD HAVE SAID SOMETHING LIKE, "THE CAPE IS THERE TO REMIND YOU THAT YOU NEVER FACE ANYTHING ALONE, THAT SOMETHING—SOMEONE—IS ALWAYS WITH YOU." IF YOU ASKED SHAZAM (THE HERO, NOT THE WIZARD), I BET HE WOULD SAY SOMETHING LIKE, "BECAUSE IT LOOKS COOL."

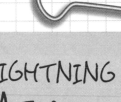

WHY DO YOU SEE LIGHTNING WHEN SHAZAM FIRST APPEARS?

AS A SUPER HERO EXPERT, THESE ARE JUST THE SORTS OF QUESTIONS I REALLY LIKE TO DIG INTO. I'VE NOTICED THAT PRIOR TO ANY APPEARANCE BY SHAZAM, A JAGGED STREAK OF LIGHTNING CRASHES THROUGH THE ATMOSPHERE, DIRECTLY INTO THE GROUND. I THINK IT HAS SOMETHING TO DO WITH HIS POWER'S VERBALLY TRIGGERED BODY MANIPULATION PROPERTIES.

KA-BOOM!

IS THERE ANYTHING SHAZAM CAN'T DO?

THERE ARE PROBABLY PLENTY OF THINGS HE CAN'T DO. AFTER A NUMBER OF TESTS, I'VE COME TO THE CONCLUSION THAT HE CAN'T TALK TO PLANTS. THE REASON I KNOW THIS IS BECAUSE ONE TIME WE WERE TESTING HIS FLYING ABILITY. AND HE FLEW RIGHT INTO A TREE. I FIGURED IF HE COULD TALK TO PLANTS, HE WOULD HAVE HEARD THE TREE SCREAMING, "HEY! YOU! THE GUY IN THE SUIT! I'M RIGHT HERE!" BUT THAT DIDN'T HAPPEN.

NOT IN THE FACE!

SUPER-QUIZ #3

LET'S SEE IF YOU WERE PAYING ATTENTION!

1. WHAT DO YOU USUALLY SEE RIGHT BEFORE SHAZAM APPEARS?
   A. BATS
   B. LIGHTNING
   C. A RAINSTORM

2. TRUE OR FALSE: THE WIZARD WHO GAVE SHAZAM HIS POWERS IS NAMED SHAZAR.
   A. TRUE
   B. FALSE

POW!

3. THE M IN SHAZAM STANDS FOR:

A. HERCULES
B. HAROLD
C. HAMBURGER

SCORING:

0-1 CORRECT: ARE YOU SURE YOU READ SECTION 3?

2 CORRECT: LOOKING GOOD. I HAVE SOME BOOKS I COULD
RECOMMEND THAT WILL HELP!

3 CORRECT: I THINK I JUST SAW LIGHTNING STRIKE!

SECTION 4
HOW TO TEST A SUPER HERO'S POWERS

ZZZO

WHILE I DON'T HAVE SUPERPOWERS MYSELF*, I WANT TO
LEARN EVERYTHING I CAN ABOUT SUPER HEROES. ESPECIALLY
SINCE I MET SHAZAM, I WANT TO BE ABLE TO HELP THEM
HOWEVER I CAN. AND ONE WAY I CAN DO THAT IS BY
HELPING THEM TEST THEIR OWN ABILITIES.

WORKING WITH SHAZAM, I'VE DEVISED A SERIES OF TESTS. THEY'RE
ESPECIALLY GOOD IF THE HERO IN QUESTION DOESN'T EXACTLY KNOW
WHAT THEIR POWERS ARE YET.

*UNLESS YOU COUNT
"KNOWING EVERYTHING
ABOUT SUPER HEROES"
AS A SUPERPOWER.**

**WHICH I DO.

IOOOOMM!

TEST #1:
FLIGHT

BECAUSE HE WAS WEARING A CAPE, IT WAS REASONABLE TO ASSUME THAT SHAZAM COULD FLY. AT LEAST, IT SEEMED REASONABLE. SURE, BATMAN WEARS A CAPE, AND HE CAN'T FLY, BUT I THINK HE'S THE EXCEPTION THAT PROVES THE RULE. CHECK OUT THE STEPS WE TOOK FOR THE FLIGHT TEST. DEFINITELY TRY THIS AT HOME.

EXPERIMENT A

I INSTRUCTED SHAZAM TO EXTEND ONE ARM, AND MAKE A FIST WITH HIS HAND. THEN PUNCH THE AIR WITH HIS FIST JUST LIKE SUPERMAN.

RESULT: NOTHING HAPPENED. HE JUST LOOKED KIND OF SILLY PUNCHING THE AIR.

EXPERIMENT B

I FORGOT THE JUMPING, OF COURSE. ONCE AGAIN, SHAZAM EXTENDED HIS ARM, MADE A FIST WITH HIS HAND, AND PUNCHED THE AIR., THIS TIME WHILE JUMPING.

RESULT: HE ACHIEVED ABOUT A QUARTER OF A SECOND OF AIR TIME, THEN GRAVITY HAPPENED. CLEARLY, SOMETHING WAS MISSING.

EXPERIMENT C

I SUGGESTED SHAZAM TRY BELIEVING HE COULD FLY. ACCORDING TO ONE PEER-REVIEWED STUDY ON SUPERPOWERS THAT I READ, BELIEF IS THE KEY TO UNLOCKING ANY ABILITY.

RESULT: SLIGHTLY BETTER RESULTS, BY WHICH I MEAN SHAZAM RAN DOWN THE STREET, RAN UP THE BACK OF A CAR, JUMPED INTO THE AIR, ACHIEVED ABOUT A HALF SECOND OF AIR TIME, THEN GRAVITY HAPPENED. AGAIN.

MAYBE WE'LL REVISIT FLIGHT.

TEST #2:
INVISIBILITY

OBVS, WE FIGURED OUT THAT SHAZAM COULD FLY, BUT
THAT CAME LATER. AFTER THE UNSUCCESSFUL FLIGHT TEST,
I THOUGHT WE'D TRY INVISIBILITY. BECAUSE THE POWER
TO REMAIN UNSEEN BY YOUR ENEMIES WOULD BE AMAZING.
EVERYBODY'S GOT ENEMIES, RIGHT?

EXPERIMENT D

TO SEE IF HE COULD RENDER HIMSELF INVISIBLE,
SHAZAM SHUT HIS EYES, AND CONCENTRATED
VERY HARD, WILLING HIMSELF TO BECOME INVISIBLE.

RESULT: IT WORKED!*

YOU'RE INVISIBLE!

I AM?!

No.

*IT DIDN'T WORK. BUT I TOTALLY FOOLED SHAZAM
INTO THINKING IT WORKED.

TEST #3:
INTELLIGENCE

ACTUALLY, THE INVISIBILITY TEST WAS THE
INTELLIGENCE TEST. AT LEAST, THAT'S WHAT I TOLD
SHAZAM. I REALLY JUST WANTED TO SEE HOW HE'D
REACT. HERE'S WHAT I FOUND OUT. THE HARD WAY.

EXPERIMENT E

WHEN I TOLD SHAZAM THAT HE WAS INVISIBLE, I ASKED WHERE
HE WAS. SO HE FLAPPED HIS ARMS (NOT UNLIKE SOME KIND OF
GIANT BIRD). THEN I BURST OUT LAUGHING. SO DID A GROUP OF
KIDS WALKING BY.

RESULT: SHAZAM GOT MAD AT ME, THREATENED ME,
AND POINTED A FINGER AT ME. BUT WHEN HE POINTED THE
FINGER, LIGHTNING SHOT FROM IT! SO BY TESTING INVISIBILITY
AND INTELLIGENCE, WE ACTUALLY DISCOVERED SHAZAM HAS
ELECTRICAL POWERS.

TEST #4:
STOPPING A BAD GUY

THIS WAS THE NEXT LOGICAL TEST. BUT IT'S NOT LIKE WE
REALLY HAD MUCH OF A CHOICE. WHILE WE WERE BUSY TESTING
ALL OF SHAZAM'S OTHER ABILITIES, WE HEARD SOMEONE
SCREAMING. WE LOOKED DOWN THE STREET AND SAW A
MUGGER TRYING TO STEAL A WOMAN'S PURSE. DON'T TRY THIS
ONE AT HOME. I MEAN, UNLESS YOUR FRIEND WANTS TO DRESS
UP LIKE A BAD GUY AND GET PEPPER-SPRAYED.

EXPERIMENT F

SHAZAM TOOK ONE LOOK AT THE BAD GUY AND HESITATED FOR A
SECOND. ONLY BECAUSE IT TOOK HIM A MINUTE TO REALIZE THAT HE
WAS A SUPER HERO, AND HAD TO GO SAVE SOMEBODY (HE WASN'T
USED TO THAT YET). HE TOOK ONE STEP, AND THE NEXT THING WE
KNEW, SHAZAM WAS RIGHT NEXT TO THE MUGGER.

RESULT: APPARENTLY OUR BOY HAS HYPER-SPEED!

EXPERIMENT 6

I THOUGHT FOR SURE THAT THIS WOULD BE THE PERFECT CHANCE FOR SHAZAM TO SEE IF HE HAD SUPER-STRENGTH OR SUPER FIGHTING ABILITIES OR SUPER-ANYTHING-LIKE-THAT. BUT WHEN HE LOOKED AT THE MUGGER, HE WAS ALREADY ON THE GROUND. AND THE SCREAMING? YEAH, THAT WAS THE MUGGER, NOT THE WOMAN. APPARENTLY SHE PEPPER-SPRAYED HIM RIGHT BEFORE SHAZAM GOT THERE.

RESULT: NO REAL NEWS HERE, BUT IT WAS PRETTY FUNNY TO HEAR SHAZAM CALL SOMEONE HIS OWN AGE "OLD."

TEST #5:
CHOOSING A NAME

OKAY, THIS ONE ISN'T REALLY A POWERS TEST. BUT ANYONE WHO TELLS YOU THAT PICKING A SUPER HERO NAME ISN'T JUST AS IMPORTANT AS FIGURING OUT YOUR POWERS IS LYING. I SHOULD ADD THAT WE WERE TRYING TO COME UP WITH A NAME BEFORE WE REALIZED THAT SHAZAM'S NAME WAS, WELL, SHAZAM.

EXPERIMENT H

I SUGGESTED SEVERAL DIFFERENT SUPER HERO NAMES. SEE CHART BELOW FOR EACH NAME, ALONG WITH SHAZAM'S REACTION.

NAME	REACTION
THUNDERCRACK	"SOUNDS LIKE A BUTT THING."
MISTER PHILADELPHIA	"SOUNDS LIKE IT'S ABOUT CREAM CHEESE."
POWER BOY	"'POWER BOY' IS NOT GONNA WORK."
CAPTAIN SPARKLEFINGERS	"THAT IS NOT MY NAME."

WE'LL COME BACK TO THIS ONE, TOO . . .

TEST #6:
REGENERATIVE HEALING

"REGENERATIVE HEALING" IS A FANCY WAY OF SAYING "HEALING YOURSELF COMPLETELY AND QUICKLY." THERE ARE DEGREES OF THIS QUICK HEALING AS WELL. FOR EXAMPLE, THE FLASH MAY HAVE REGENERATIVE HEALING BUT THAT IS MAINLY BECAUSE EVERYTHING IN HIS BODY MOVES QUICKER THAN A NORMAL HUMAN. SO THAT WOULD INCLUDE HIS ABILITY TO HEAL. BUT WHAT ABOUT SHAZAM?

EXPERIMENT I

SHAZAM AND I WERE IN A CONVENIENCE STORE, CONDUCTING ANOTHER COMPLETELY UNRELATED TEST*, WHEN WE SAW TWO PEOPLE TRYING TO ROB THE CASH REGISTER. SHAZAM MOVED QUICKLY AND GRABBED A ROBBER'S PISTOL BEFORE THEY EVEN KNEW WHAT WAS HAPPENING. BUT THE SECOND ROBBER GOT OFF A SHOT. TOO BAD FOR HIM, THE BULLET HIT SHAZAM'S CHEST, FLATTENED, AND FELL TO THE FLOOR. OKAY, SO THIS DIDN'T REALLY TEST HIS ABILITY TO HEAL BUT NOW WE KNOW—HE DOESN'T HAVE TO!

RESULT: ADD BULLETPROOF TO THE POWER MIX!

*SEEING WHAT WE COULD BUY IN A CONVENIENCE STORE.

TEST #7:
FIRE IMMUNITY

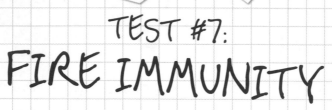

REMEMBER WHEN I MENTIONED THE THING ABOUT
HABANERO JERKY? WELL, I'M MENTIONING IT AGAIN
BECAUSE AFTER SHAZAM STOPPED THE ROBBERY AT THE
CONVENIENCE STORE, WE GOT A WHOLE TON OF HABANERO
JERKY TO EAT. NOT A LITERAL TON, BUT PRETTY CLOSE.

EXPERIMENT J

I THOUGHT THIS WOULD BE A GOOD TIME TO ADD FIRE TO THE MIX. BUT
INSTEAD SHAZAM AND I JUST HUNG OUT AND ATE A TON OF HABANERO
JERKY. SAME THING, RIGHT?

RESULT: WE DIDN'T REALLY TEST HIS FIRE IMMUNITY WITH "FLAMES"
BUT THE SMELL THAT CAME LATER . . . LET'S MOVE ON.

TEST #8:
ABILITY TO TALK TO FISH

After everything I'd already seen, I was pretty sure that Shazam most likely wouldn't have this ability. But hey, worth a shot! Aquaman can do it! Maybe Shazam is some sort of electric eel. Also maybe at this point, I'm just messing with him.

EXPERIMENT K

Shazam and I were in my room when I told him to take the fish bowl and concentrate very hard. Be the fish. Know the fish. Talk to the fish. CONTROL the fish. He stared at the bowl for a long time and I burst out laughing.

RESULT: I was tackled to the ground. The fish is okay though.

TEST #9:
HEAT VISION

I KNOW, YOU'RE GOING TO SAY, "FREDDY, ARE YOU
OBSESSED WITH SUPERMAN?" SURE, BIG RED HAS HEAT
VISION, BUT THAT'S JUST HIM, RIGHT? WELL, YOU DON'T
KNOW UNTIL YOU TRY. AND IF HE DIDN'T HAVE HEAT VISION,
MAYBE SHAZAM HAD SOME OTHER KIND OF OCULAR ABILITY?

EXPERIMENT L
I TOLD SHAZAM I HAD ANOTHER TEST IN MIND. THE HEAT-VISION TEST. I
TOLD HIM TO STARE AT A NEARBY BENCH AS HARD AS HE COULD, AND THINK
HOT THOUGHTS.

RESULT: HE PUNCHED ME, AND NOW I HAVE DEAD ARM.

EXPERIMENT M

With no sign of heat vision, I figured we'd see if he had microscopic vision—like, could he see something really tiny? I told him to stare at a drop of water and see if he could see all the single-celled animals living within. He stared at the drop as hard as he could, and thought small thoughts.

RESULT: He punched me, and now I have dead arm in the other arm.

TEST #10:
DUPLICATING POWERS

I WANTED TO SEE IF SHAZAM COULD CONJURE MULTIPLES OF SOMETHING. I THINK AT THIS POINT WE WERE JUST HUNGRY.

EXPERIMENT N

I GOT A PIE FROM THE CONVENIENCE STORE AND TOLD SHAZAM TO CONCENTRATE ON THE PIE. THINK MORE PIE. PIE. PIE. PIES.

RESULT: NOTHING. NO DUPLICATING POWERS. WE WERE SO BUMMED WE WENT BACK TO THE STORE AND BOUGHT A BUNCH OF PIES TO MAKE US FEEL BETTER.

SUPER-QUIZ #4

I HOPE YOU WERE READING EVERY SINGLE WORD OF THE LAST SECTION. BECAUSE NOW'S YOUR CHANCE TO SHOW WHAT YOU KNOW!

1. WHICH OF THE FOLLOWING IS NOT ONE OF SHAZAM'S POWERS?
   A. FLIGHT
   B. SUPER-STRENGTH
   C. HYPER-ORIGAMI

2. WHAT WAS THE MUGGER DOING WHEN SHAZAM WENT TO STOP HIM?
   A. SCREAMING FROM THE PEPPER SPRAY IN HIS EYES
   B. LAUGHING AT SHAZAM'S OUTRAGEOUS COSTUME
   C. SNEEZING FROM THE WOMAN'S BANANA-SCENTED PERFUME

3. STOMACH INVULNERABILITY—IS IT A THING?
   A. YES, IT'S A THING.
   B. NO, IT'S NOT A THING.
   C. IT SHOULD BE A THING.

ANSWERS: 1. C, 2. A, 3. B AND C

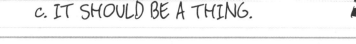

0-1 CORRECT: I'M GONNA GUESS YOUR SUPERPOWER ISN'T MEMORIZING SHAZAM'S SUPERPOWERS.

2 CORRECT: YOU'RE REALLY GETTING THE HANG OF THIS SUPER HERO BUSINESS!

3 CORRECT: LET'S COUNT SUPER-MEMORY AS ONE OF YOUR POWERS!

SECTION 5

HOW DO THEY STACK UP?

WE'VE ALREADY TALKED ABOUT THE WHOLE WHO'S FASTER, SUPERMAN OR SHAZAM? THING. BUT THAT'S THE STUFF THAT EVERYONE REALLY WANTS TO KNOW. THAT'S WHAT I REALLY WANT TO KNOW. ESPECIALLY BECAUSE SHAZAM IS MY FRIEND! I WANT TO KNOW EXACTLY HOW HIS POWERS STACK UP AGAINST THE OTHER HEROES'. WHO KNOWS, MAYBE ONE DAY SHAZAM WILL BE ASKED TO JOIN THE JUSTICE LEAGUE. AND BECAUSE OF MY RESEARCH, WE'LL KNOW JUST WHAT HE CAN DO TO HELP!

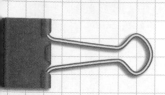

COOL CLOTHES

FIRST THINGS FIRST. BEFORE WE EVEN GET INTO THE POWERS, WE HAVE TO COMPARE COSTUMES. AND LET ME JUST SAY, I THINK SHAZAM WINS THIS ONE HANDS DOWN. I MEAN, LOOK AT THAT SUIT! IT'S CLASSIC! THAT LIGHTNING BOLT, SO ICONIC! LIKE, SUPERMAN-LEVEL ICONIC!

OF COURSE, I EXPECT BATMAN WOULD DISAGREE. . . .

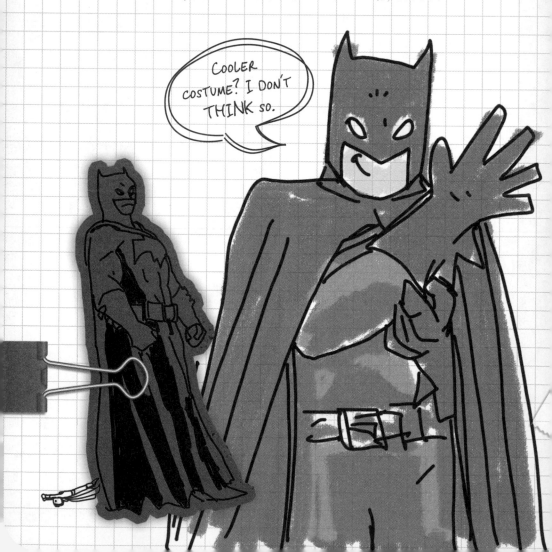

COOLER COSTUME? I DON'T THINK SO.

STRENGTH

THERE ARE SOME REAL HEAVY HITTERS IN THE JUSTICE LEAGUE. WITH THE LEVEL OF THREATS THEY FACE, THERE WOULD HAVE TO BE, WOULDN'T THERE? SO HOW DOES SHAZAM LOOK AGAINST THIS KIND OF COMPETITION?

WELL, SUPERMAN AND WONDER WOMAN ARE IN A CLASS BY THEMSELVES. IT'S HARD TO SAY WHICH OF THEM IS STRONGER. I THINK SUPERMAN HAS THE EDGE, THOUGH. BASED ON THE AVAILABLE EVIDENCE, I THINK SHAZAM MIGHT BE MORE POWERFUL THAN AQUAMAN OR CYBORG. HE'S CERTAINLY STRONGER THAN BATMAN OR THE FLASH.

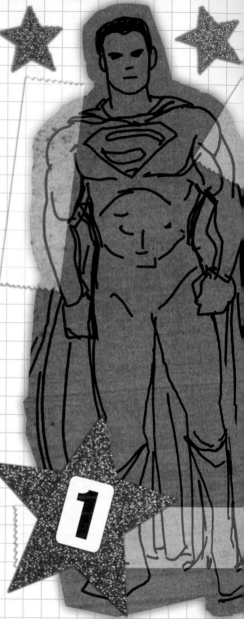

1

WHO DO YOU THINK IS THE STRONGEST? RANK THE HEROES YOURSELF!

RANK

SUPERMAN	WONDER WOMAN	SHAZAM

2

3

4

5

6

7

AQUAMAN   CYBORG   BATMAN   THE FLASH

SPEED

We've already talked about speed a little bit. But if we're really going to get into it, we have to analyze each super hero's real abilities in this area.

First and foremost, the Flash is a speed champ. He lives, breathes, and eats speed. Maybe hot dogs, too. So he's gotta be number one. But Superman is right up there, too. Then I think you have to give it to Shazam. He can fly super fast; he's got that hyper-speed I talked about earlier. Plus, he's still new—who knows, he may end up being faster than anyone!

1

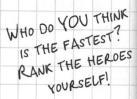
Who do you think is the fastest? Rank the heroes yourself!

SUPERMAN  WONDER WOMAN  SHAZAM

 RANK

AQUAMAN   CYBORG   BATMAN   THE FLASH

INTELLIGENCE

This is one of the most important areas for any hero. It's great to have powers, but you need the smarts to know how—and when—to use them.

Right away, I'm going to put Batman in the number one slot. He's a master planner, master strategist, master you-name-it. Wonder Woman and Cyborg aren't far behind. Wonder Woman's got a super-brain like a computer, and Cyborg's brain might very well BE a computer!

But what about Shazam? I'll be honest. He is awesome. But the jury's still out on the smarts department! Hopefully he figures out how to tap into that Wisdom of Solomon eventually.

Who do you think is the smartest? Rank the heroes yourself!

RANK

SUPERMAN	WONDER WOMAN	SHAZAM

AQUAMAN CYBORG BATMAN THE FLASH

FIGHTING ABILITY

1

THROW ANY OF THESE HEROES INTO THE MIDDLE OF A KNOCK-DOWN, DRAG-OUT FIGHT, AND THEY'RE GOING TO COME OUT ON TOP. BUT WHO'S GOT THE BEST BATTLE MOVES?

I'M PRETTY SURE THAT NO ONE CAN BEAT WONDER WOMAN. SHE'S BEEN FIGHTING SINCE SHE WAS A KID, AND SHE'S BEEN AROUND FOR A REALLY LONG TIME. SHE'S LEARNED EVERY STYLE OF COMBAT, AND ISN'T AFRAID TO USE IT. BATMAN'S RIGHT BEHIND HER, THOUGH.

THE DARK KNIGHT IS A QUICK STUDY! AQUAMAN'S A REAL BRUISER, AND THEN THERE'S SUPERMAN.

SHAZAM? WELL, HE'S STILL LEARNING. BUT ONCE HE GETS UP TO SPEED, HE'LL GIVE EVERYONE A RUN FOR THEIR MONEY!

WHO DO YOU THINK IS THE BEST FIGHTER? RANK THE HEROES YOURSELF!

 RANK

SUPERMAN	WONDER WOMAN	SHAZAM

AQUAMAN

CYBORG

BATMAN

THE FLASH

TECHNOLOGY

This one is more cut-and-dried than the others, but only because some of these heroes don't rely on tech at all.

Cyborg is clearly the winner. He's an example of how perfectly people and technology can interact and achieve a kind of symbiosis. Right behind him is Batman, whose own ability to create gadgets (and GIZMOS!) is pretty impressive.

Shazam? Yeah, no gizmos, no gadgets, no tech. But he looks good in that suit!

1

Who do YOU think is the most tech savvy? Rank the heroes yourself!

SUPERMAN	WONDER WOMAN	SHAZAM

RANK

AQUAMAN CYBORG  BATMAN THE FLASH

POWER...
TO HAVE FUN!

OKAY, TECHNICALLY NOT A
SUPERPOWER. BUT HAVING FUN IS
IMPORTANT. I KNOW THIS,
BECAUSE I'M A KID.

YOU KNOW WHO ELSE KNOWS THIS? AH, SHAZAM,
THAT'S WHO. THAT'S WHY HE'S NUMBER ONE!
THE FLASH IS ALSO PRETTY COOL, AND I THINK
AQUAMAN IS, TOO. SO'S WONDER WOMAN, FOR
THAT MATTER. AND SUPERMAN. I
DON'T KNOW MUCH ABOUT CYBORG,
BUT I'LL GIVE HIM THE
BENEFIT OF THE DOUBT.

BUT ONE THING I DO
KNOW—I CAN THINK OF
A THOUSAND WORDS TO
DESCRIBE BATMAN, BUT
"FUN" ISN'T ONE OF THEM.

WHO DO YOU THINK
IS THE MOST FUN?
RANK THE HEROES
YOURSELF!

SUPERMAN	WONDER WOMAN	SHAZAM

 RANK

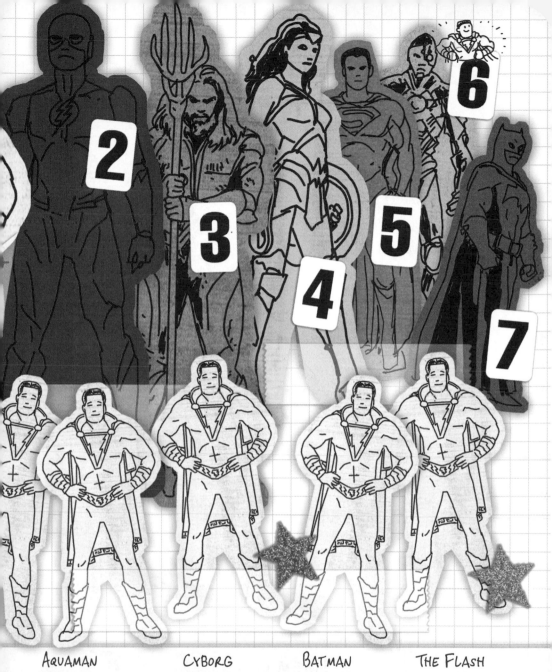

AQUAMAN CYBORG BATMAN THE FLASH

SUPER-QUIZ #5

WE JUST PITTED HERO AGAINST HERO TO SEE WHO WAS THE MOST POWERFUL. NOW PIT YOUR BRAIN AGAINST THESE QUESTIONS! GOOD LUCK, YOUR BRAIN!

1. ACCORDING TO FREDDY FREEMAN, WHO'S THE SMARTEST?
   A. BATMAN
   B. SHAZAM
   C. WONDER WOMAN

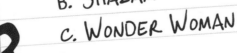

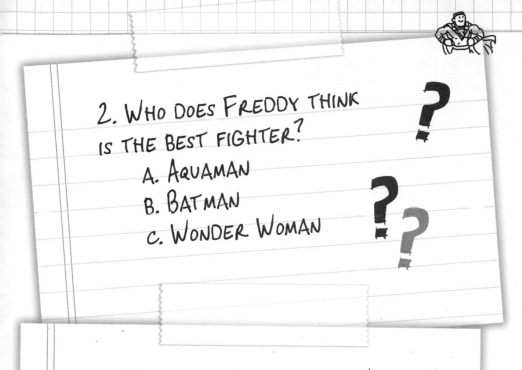

2. WHO DOES FREDDY THINK IS THE BEST FIGHTER?
   A. AQUAMAN
   B. BATMAN
   C. WONDER WOMAN

3. WHO IS CLEARLY THE MOST FUN?
   A. SHAZAM
   B. SHAZAM
   C. SHAZAM

1. A, 2. C, 3. A, B, AND C, OBVS

SCORING:

0–1 CORRECT: ARE YOU SURE YOU'RE NOT SECRETLY LEX LUTHOR?

2 CORRECT: YOU'RE MOVING UP!

3 CORRECT: YOU'RE THE BEST—AT TAKING MY QUIZZES!

SECTION 6

EVERYTHING I KNOW I LEARNED FROM SHAZAM, EXCEPT NOT EVERYTHING, BUT SOME THINGS FOR SURE

I'VE WRITTEN SO MUCH ABOUT SUPER HEROES, BUT
I WANTED TO SAY A FEW THINGS THAT I LEARNED
FROM HANGING OUT WITH SHAZAM.

AND I'M NOT TALKING ABOUT HOW TO SUPER-BURP,
ALTHOUGH I DID LEARN THAT.

IT WAS AWESOME.

BEST ★
Friends
FOREVER

JUST BECAUSE YOU CAN DO A THING DOESN'T MEAN YOU SHOULD DO A THING

When you have all those powers like Shazam, it's really easy to forget that using them can sometimes cause disaster. Sure, they're great for helping people. But if you don't stop to think first, you might end up hurting somebody by accident.

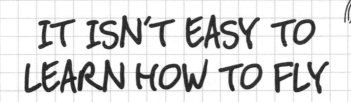

IT ISN'T EASY TO LEARN HOW TO FLY

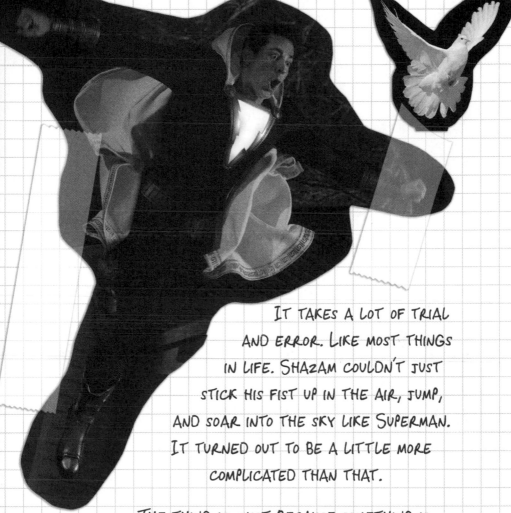

IT TAKES A LOT OF TRIAL AND ERROR. LIKE MOST THINGS IN LIFE. SHAZAM COULDN'T JUST STICK HIS FIST UP IN THE AIR, JUMP, AND SOAR INTO THE SKY LIKE SUPERMAN. IT TURNED OUT TO BE A LITTLE MORE COMPLICATED THAN THAT.

THE THING IS, JUST BECAUSE SOMETHING IS DIFFICULT, IT DOESN'T MEAN YOU SHOULD QUIT. IT JUST MEANS THAT YOU SHOULD TRY EVEN HARDER.

BECAUSE YOU ARE GOOD. AND YOU GOT THIS.

BE YOURSELF

You can try to act like someone else, someone tougher, or stronger, or cooler, but guess what? At the end of the day, you're YOU. And there's only one of you. So you can spend all your time trying to be a different person, or you can be the best YOU there is.

Just like Shazam. He never pretended to be anything other than what he was. He's kinda goofy, and a little weird, and I wouldn't want him any other way.

POW!

HAVING SUPERPOWERS
IS AWESOME

THIS IS PRETTY SELF-EXPLANATORY. BECAUSE
YOU KNOW WHAT?

HAVING SUPERPOWERS IS
AWESOME.

ENOUGH SAID.

CAPES ARE COOL

I MEAN, I ALREADY KNEW THIS FROM ALL
MY RESEARCH ON SUPERMAN. THAT GUY CAN
REALLY WEAR A CAPE. BUT SHAZAM REALLY
SHOWED ME THAT CAPES ARE COOL.

HE COULD HAVE LOOKED SO DOOFY WITH THAT
THING, BUT HE DOESN'T!
HE JUST HAS THIS LOOK LIKE, HEY, SHOULDN'T
YOU BE WEARING A CAPE, TOO?

FRIENDS TO THE END

YOU NEVER KNOW WHO YOU MIGHT BECOME FRIENDS WITH. IT MIGHT BE SOME KID YOU JUST MET, OR A SUPER HERO WHO SHOWS UP WITH A BOLT OF LIGHTNING. EITHER WAY, YOU'RE LUCKY. AND THEY'RE LUCKY, TOO.

YOU'RE *my* BEST FRIEND

SUPER QUIZ #6

JUST KIDDING! THERE IS NO
SUPER-QUIZ #6. INSTEAD, I
HAVE A MESSAGE TO YOU FROM
SHAZAM HIMSELF.

DEAR PERSON READING THIS
RIGHT NOW,

WASN'T THIS COOL? FREDDY DID
AN AMAZING JOB. LET'S GIVE IT
UP FOR FREDDY!

(ALSO, DON'T TELL HIM THAT I
ATE THAT BAG OF CORN CHIPS,
OKAY? SERIOUSLY, I DIDN'T
KNOW IT WAS FROM THE
STORE THAT SUPERMAN SAVED!
PROBABLY EXPLAINS WHY THEY
TASTED KINDA STALE.)

BE COOL, STAY IN SCHOOL,

SHAZAM

SECTION 7

CAN I BE A SUPER HERO LIKE SHAZAM?

Take it from an expert—anyone can be a super hero. Maybe not like Shazam, exactly. Sure, having powers helps, and having cool gadgets (AND GIZMOS!) like the Batmobile doesn't hurt, either. But you don't necessarily NEED those things, either. One thing I've learned from hanging out with Shazam is that you have everything you already need right inside you.

And if that sounds corny, well, it is. But it's also TRUE.

MY FOSTER SIBLINGS HELP ME SEE WHAT'S RIGHT INSIDE ME
(MAINLY CORN CHIPS AND BEEF JERKY).

PURE OF HEART, STRONG IN SPIRIT

THIS IS SOMETHING THAT THE WIZARD SHAZAM SAID TO THE SUPER HERO SHAZAM. HE WAS LOOKING FOR A PERSON, SOMEONE WHO HAD A STRONG SPIRIT AND A PURE HEART.

THAT PERSON BECAME THE SUPER HERO SHAZAM. WHAT THE WIZARD MEANT WAS, HE COULDN'T TRUST SUCH INCREDIBLE POWERS WITH JUST ANYBODY. THE PERSON HAD TO BE TRULY GOOD. THEY COULDN'T BE SELFISH OR WANT POWER JUST FOR THE SAKE OF HAVING IT, BECAUSE IT'S COOL OR WHATEVER. THEY HAD TO HAVE THE SOUL OF A HERO.

(AGAIN, CORNY BUT TRUE.)

SET AN EXAMPLE

If you want to be a super hero in your everyday life, you have to learn to set an example. Take Superman, for instance. Sure, he can probably move a mountain with his bare hands. But that isn't the thing that makes everyone look up to him.

No, people look up to Superman because he tries his best all the time. He tries to be the best Superman he can be. And that's a lesson for all of us. If we all tried to be a little more like Superman, the world would be a better place.

BE BRAVE

Let's face it, life can be pretty intense.
It can be scary. And sometimes you feel
like you're all alone. But you know what?
You're not. If you look around, I'll bet you
find people who really care about you. And
you probably care about them, too. There's
strength in that. You can take courage
from it.

It allows you to be brave.
And with power like that,
you can face
anything.

TAKE RISKS

I'm not talking about risks that could get you hurt or get you into trouble. I mean, I know a thing or two about getting in trouble, and I can't recommend it. But I can recommend taking risks—the kind of risks that put you out there, where you take a chance on something new or something you're not sure about.

Maybe it's talking to a new kid at school for the first time. Or reading a book that seems really challenging. Or learning how to play a sport you never tried before.

Try something new. Take a chance.

LOOK OUT FOR EACH OTHER

I SAID IT BEFORE, AND I'LL SAY IT AGAIN. YOU'RE NOT IN THIS ALONE. IF YOU LOOK HARD ENOUGH, YOU'LL FIND YOU HAVE PEOPLE IN YOUR CORNER. PEOPLE WHO WILL FIGHT FOR YOU. WHO WILL DO ANYTHING FOR YOU. AND YOU'LL DO THE SAME THING FOR THEM.

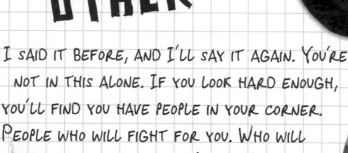

THAT MAKES EACH OF US HEROES. OUR WILLINGNESS TO GO ABOVE AND BEYOND TO HELP EACH OTHER.

AND IT'S NOT JUST PEOPLE WE KNOW. WE'RE THERE TO HELP COMPLETE STRANGERS, TOO. WE'RE ALL CONNECTED. IF WE CAN HELP PEOPLE WE KNOW AND PEOPLE WE DON'T KNOW, WE'RE ALL ON OUR WAY TO BECOMING SUPER HEROES.

NEVER STOP LEARNING

A REAL HERO KNOWS THERE IS MUCH THAT THEY DON'T KNOW. AND THEY KEEP ON LEARNING, TRYING TO ABSORB AS MUCH KNOWLEDGE AS THEY CAN. LOOK AT GUYS LIKE THE FLASH—HE'S JUST LEARNING ABOUT ALL THE COOL THINGS HE CAN DO WITH HIS SPEED. OR CYBORG. YOU CAN BET THAT HE'S ALWAYS MAKING UPGRADES TO HIS OPERATING SYSTEMS, AND COMING UP WITH ALL KINDS OF AMAZING GIZMOS.
(AND GADGETS!)

THAT'S PROBABLY WHY I READ SO MUCH, AND STUDY SUPER HEROES EVERY CHANCE I GET. I WANT TO LEARN EVERYTHING I CAN ABOUT THEM.
BECAUSE, AND THIS IS GONNA SOUND
MAJOR CORNY,
KNOWLEDGE IS POWER.

NEVER GIVE UP

THERE ARE GOING TO BE TIMES WHERE EVERYTHING SEEMS HOPELESS. I KNOW I'VE FELT THAT WAY SOMETIMES. BUT THE THING IS, SUPER HEROES DON'T GIVE IN TO THAT FEELING. THEY DON'T JUST GIVE UP WHEN THE GOING GETS ROUGH.

THEY PICK THEMSELVES UP OFF THE GROUND, STAND UP, AND GIVE IT THEIR BEST SHOT. OVER AND OVER AND OVER AGAIN. DO YOU THINK BATMAN EVER JUST GIVES UP? OR WONDER WOMAN JUST STOPS FIGHTING? NOT GONNA HAPPEN.

AND WE CAN'T GIVE UP, EITHER. BECAUSE THE TRUE MEASURE OF A HERO IS STANDING UP WHEN THE ODDS ARE AGAINST YOU.

SUPER-QUIZ #7

You've reached the end of Section 7, so you know what that means! Are you ready?

1. Which of the following is NOT important to being a super hero?
   - A. Not giving up
   - B. Being brave
   - C. Staying home and watching TV

2. Complete this phrase: Pure of heart, strong in
   - A. Spit
   - B. Spirit
   - C. Sprinting

3. I STILL THINK THAT CORN CHIPS ARE BETTER THAN POTATO CHIPS.

    A. THAT'S NOT A QUESTION.

    B. WHY ARE WE STILL ON THIS?

    C. WELL, YOU'RE WRONG.

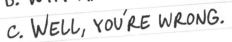

SCORING:

0-1 CORRECT: LET'S TRY THIS AGAIN, SHALL WE?

2 CORRECT: YOU HAVE THE MAKINGS OF A TRUE HERO.

3 CORRECT: SOMEONE CALL THE JUSTICE LEAGUE—WE HAVE A NEW MEMBER!

My other fibling (foster sibling) Mary felt the need to give me all of her quizzes from this book. SHOW-OFF.

SUPER QUIZ #1

1. b
2. c

SUPER QUIZ #2

1. b
2. b
3. a

WINNER!
100%

SUPER QUIZ #3

1. c   2. a
3. b and c

BIG NEWS.

Lois Lane (THE LOIS LANE) wrote me back!!!
She said I could send in a writing sample (she liked
   my writing!) and she would read it and
      MAYBE JUST MAYBE publish it
         in the newspaper.
      AND GUESS WHAT (drumroll please.........)
         THEY PUBLISHED MY ARTICLE!!

No big deal, BUT I'm pretty much a celebrity now.

Daily Planet

What Makes a Hero?

By Freddy Freeman

Everyday, thousands of heroes in all shapes and sizes, colors and backgrounds walk amongst us. They can be neighbors, teachers, moms, dads, and even best friends. They are the people that lend a hand when you need one.

(continued on pag

[article continued]

They are the brothers and sisters that always are there to help you when you need it the most. Heroes are all around us. Trying to do the right thing, even when they are faced with a lot of bad things. When I wrote my soon-to-be-*New-York-Times*-bestseller *Freddy's Guide to Super Hero-ing*, I learned that wearing a cape, having a super hero name, and being able to fly or lift mountains was just half of what makes a super hero. The other part to being a super hero was what was inside, what was underneath that cape. And no matter how cool your hair is, or how awesome your name sounds when yelled out loud, if you don't have the heart, courage, and desire to fight, to keep going forward, no matter what stands in your way and what mountain blocks you from moving forward, you're just a person in a cape. With cool hair. So look around. Find that hero. They could be right next to you. And who knows: that hero could be you.

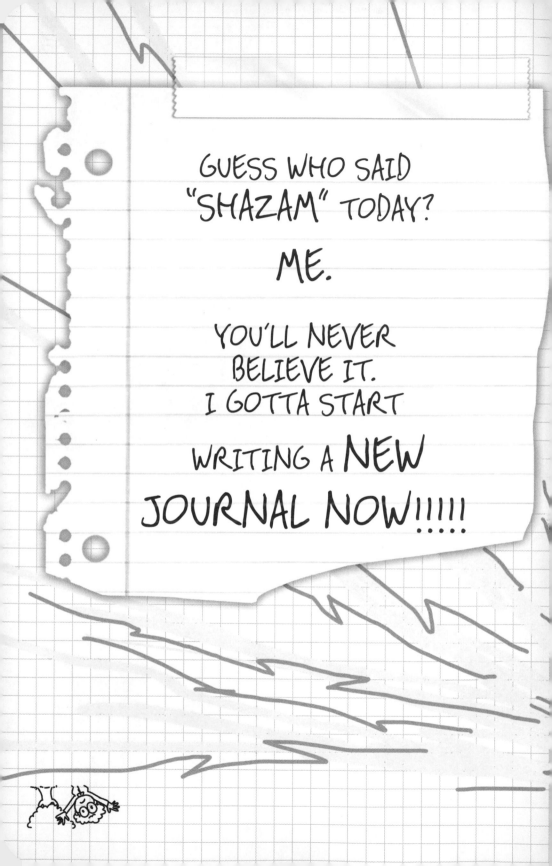

WHAT ARE YOU WAITING FOR? AN INVITIATION?
WELL, HERE IT IS! WRITE IN HERE LIKE IT'S YOUR
OWN JOURNAL . . . OR LIKE IT'S YOUR BIRTHDAY.

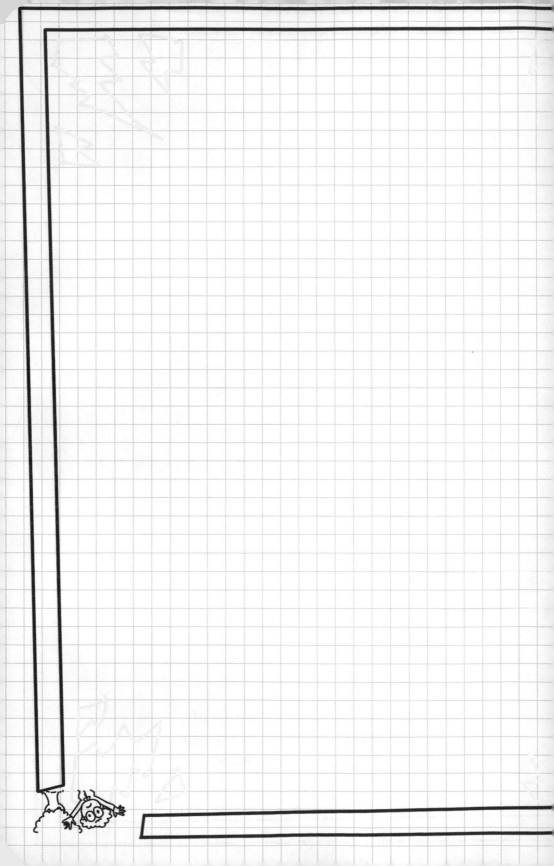

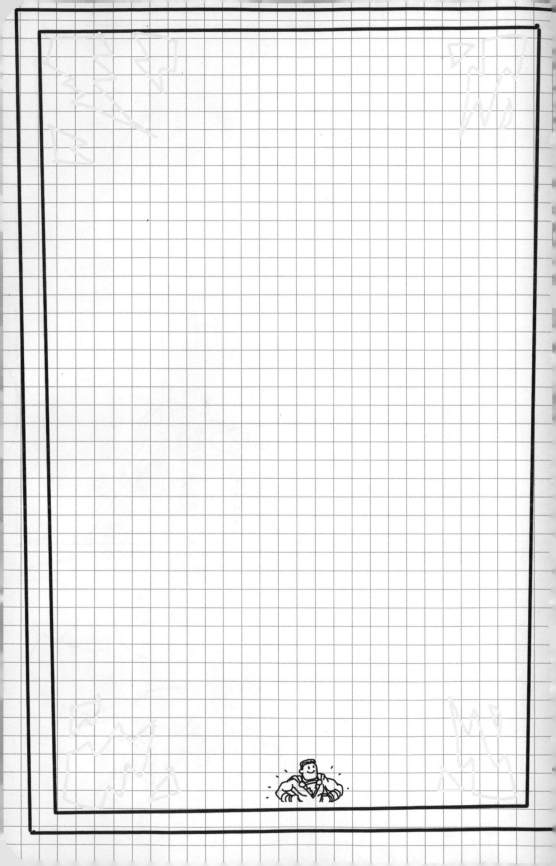